Lettice

For Ruby & Moss, our bunny girls xx

First published in hardback in Great Britain by HarperCollins Children's Books in 2006
First published in paperback in 2006

3 5 7 9 10 8 6 4 2
ISBN-13: 978-0-00-718409-5

HarperCollins Children's Books is a division of HarperCollins Publishers Ltd.

Text and illustrations copyright © Mandy Stanley 2006

The author/illustrator asserts the moral right to be identified as the author/illustrator of the work.
A CIP catalogue record for this title is available from the British Library.

Visit our website at: www.harpercollinschildrensbooks.co.uk

Printed and bound in China

Lettice

The Birthday Party

Mandy Stanley

HarperCollins *Children's Books*

Lettice Rabbit and her family lived high up on top of a hill. Nibble, nibble, hop, hop, every day was the same, until one afternoon...

Lettice peeped out of the burrow
and saw a little girl with wings,
chasing a balloon.

Lettice scampered after the little girl and
soon she saw a mum and four more children.
'Hello!' said the little girl. 'I'm Jasmine.
It's my birthday party.
Want to join in?'

Lettice didn't need to be asked twice.
She couldn't wait to find out what
happened at a birthday party.

First they played leap frog. Lettice was good at that!

Then they played catch...

...and then
hide and seek.

Next Jasmine opened her birthday presents.
There was a butterfly kite...

a pink
skipping rope,

...and a beautiful princess doll
with lots of different dresses.

But something was
bothering Lettice.

Shyly, she said,
'I wish I had something
special to wear, like you.'

Jasmine held out one of her
doll's dresses. 'You can have this!' she said.
'Can I?' whispered Lettice.

Very carefully,
she stepped into the
tiny dress and shoes.

Jasmine placed a sparkly tiara over
Lettice's ears. It fitted perfectly!
Lettice was a princess!

'Now let's have tea,'
said Jasmine's mum.

But, just then, a drop of rain fell on the cake.
'Oh, no!' cried Jasmine. 'It can't rain. Not today!'

'My birthday is *ruined!*' wept Jasmine.
Lettice was upset. What could she do?

Then Lettice
had an idea.

'Come on everyone,
follow me!'
she said.

And she led the way...

...to a beautiful secret glade,
where the trees arched over
and kept out the rain.

It was truly magical.

They lit the candles on the cake
and everyone sang Happy Birthday.

Jasmine blew
out the candles
and made a
secret wish.

After tea, Lettice
peeped outside.
'Look!' she said.
'It's stopped raining.'

Later, on the way home,
they flew the new kite...

...and just as they came to the bottom
of the hill, there was a rainbow.

'Thank you for making this the best
birthday ever!' said Jasmine,
holding out a party bag.
'For me?' blushed Lettice. 'Oh, thank you!'

Lettice waved
goodbye...

...and rushed home to share her
goodies with the family.

The bag was full of pretty things.
Lettice's favourite was a very special balloon.